Smallpox
Carmel Reilly

Smallpox

Fast Forward
Turquoise Level 18

Text: Carmel Reilly
Editor: Johanna Rohan
Design: Vonda Pestana
Series design: James Lowe
Production controller: Seona Galbally
Photo research: Corrina Tauschke
Audio recordings: Juliet Hill, Picture Start
Spoken by: Matthew King and Abbe Holmes
Reprint: Siew Han Ong

Acknowledgements
The author and publisher would like to acknowledge permission to reproduce material from the following sources:

Photographs by APL/Corbis/Seattle Post-Intelligencer Collection; Museum of History and Industry, p20; Getty Images/ Hulton Archive, p10; Getty Images/ Reportage/Koichi Kamoshida, p4 bottom; Getty Images/ Reportage/ Per-Anders Pettersson, p4 top; Getty Images/ Reportage/Tom Stoddart Archive, p22; Getty Images/The Bridgeman Art Library/ Giuseppe Bonito, p11; Getty Images/ Time Life Pictures/ Terrence Spencer, pp front cover, 1, 6; Getty Images/ Visuals Unlimited/Dr FA Murphy, pp 3, 9 left; Getty Images/Visuals Unlimited/ Science VU/CDC, p9 right; iStockphoto.com, pp 6-9, back cover; iStockphoto.com/José Carlos Pires Pereira, p12 bottom left; iStockphoto.com/Russell Tate, p19; Photolibrary/ Bsip/LA/ Tevybattini, p7; Photolibrary/ Photo Researchers Inc, pp 8, 12 centre left; Photolibrary/ Photo Researchers Inc/ David Davis, p7 top; Photolibrary/ Science Photo Library, p17; Photolibrary/ Science Photo Library/ Jean-Loup Charmet, pp. 14, 16; Photolibrary/ Science Photo Library/ National Library of Medicine, pp. 13, 15, 18; Photolibrary/ Science Photo Library/ Saturn Stills, pp 23 centre, 23 bottom; Photolibrary/ Science Photo Library/Tek Image, pp5 bottom, 23 top; Photolibrary/ Science Photolibrary/ Sotiris Zafeiris, p5 top; World Health Organization/ Centre for Disease Control & Prevention, p21.

ISBN 978 0 17 012640 3
ISBN 978 0 17 012633 5 (set)

Cengage Learning Australia
Level 7, 80 Dorcas Street
South Melbourne, Victoria Australia 3205
Phone: 1300 790 853

Cengage Learning New Zealand
Unit 4B Rosedale Office Park
331 Rosedale Road, Albany, North Shore NZ 0632
Phone: 0800 449 725

For learning solutions, visit **cengage.com.au**

Printed in Australia by Ligare Pty Ltd
4 5 6 7 8 9 10 23 22 21 20 19

Evaluated in independent research by staff from the
Department of Language, Literacy and Arts Education
at the University of Melbourne.

Smallpox

Carmel Reilly

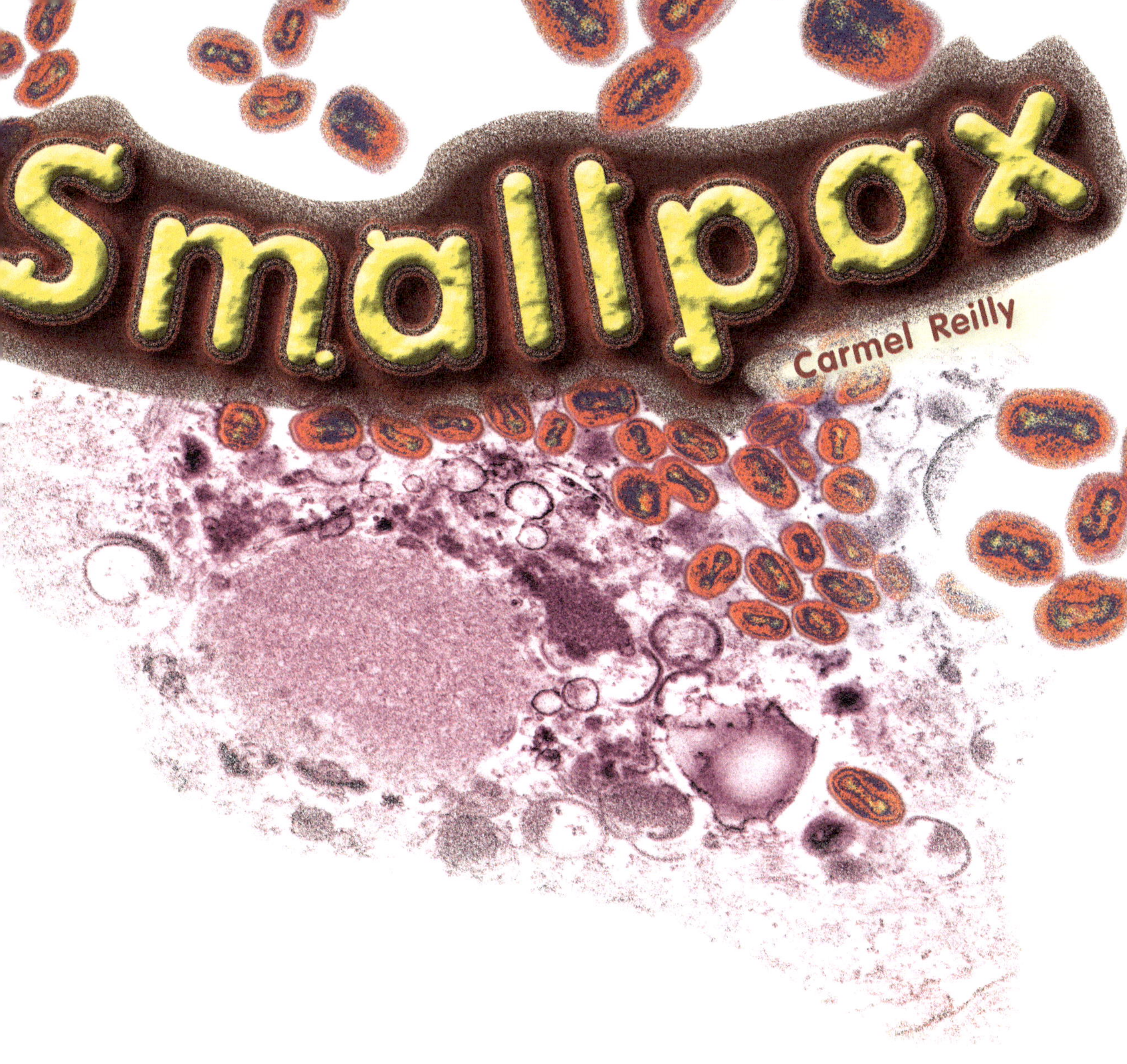

Contents

Chapter 1

THE BIGGEST CHALLENGE

People have always faced huge challenges. Over time, war, famine and accidents have taken millions of lives.

But, the biggest challenge people have faced has always been **disease**.

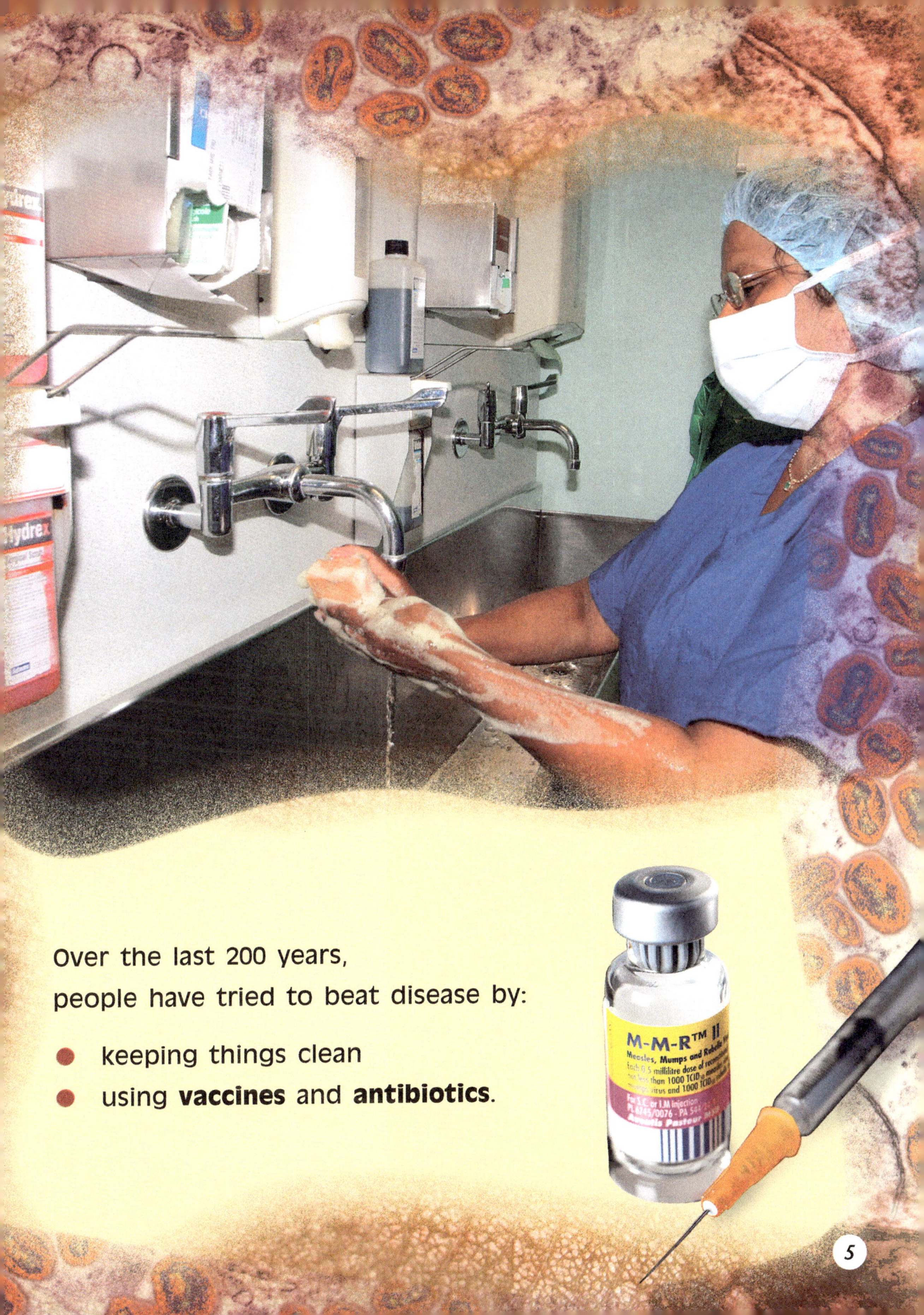

Over the last 200 years,
people have tried to beat disease by:

- keeping things clean
- using **vaccines** and **antibiotics**.

Chapter 2

SMALLPOX

Vaccination was one of the first big steps in beating disease.
The first vaccine made was for smallpox.

Smallpox was one of the most terrible diseases in history.
Smallpox killed millions of people all over the world, and millions more were blinded or left with terrible scars.

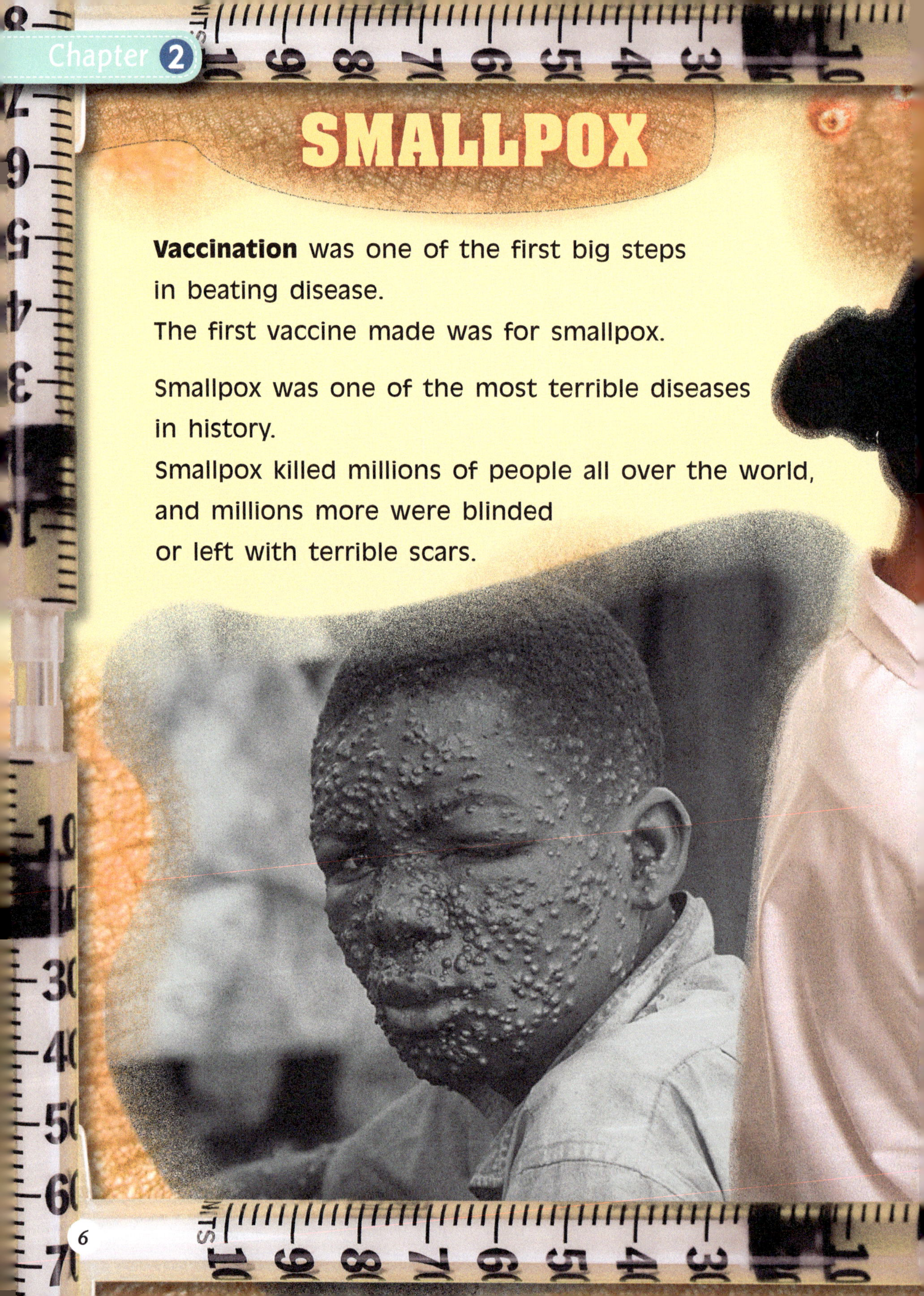

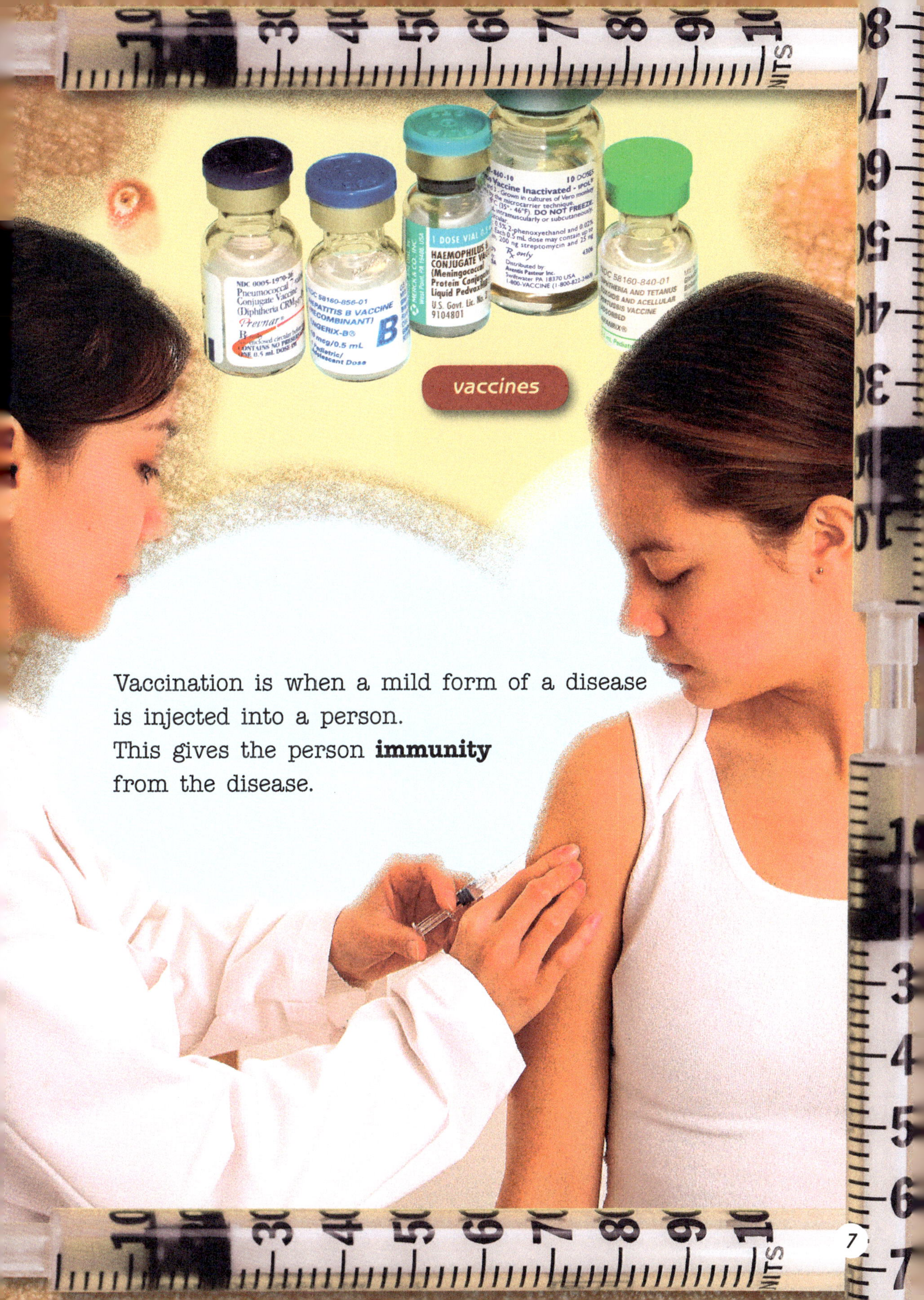

Vaccination is when a mild form of a disease is injected into a person.
This gives the person **immunity** from the disease.

There has not been a case of smallpox in the world for the last 30 years.

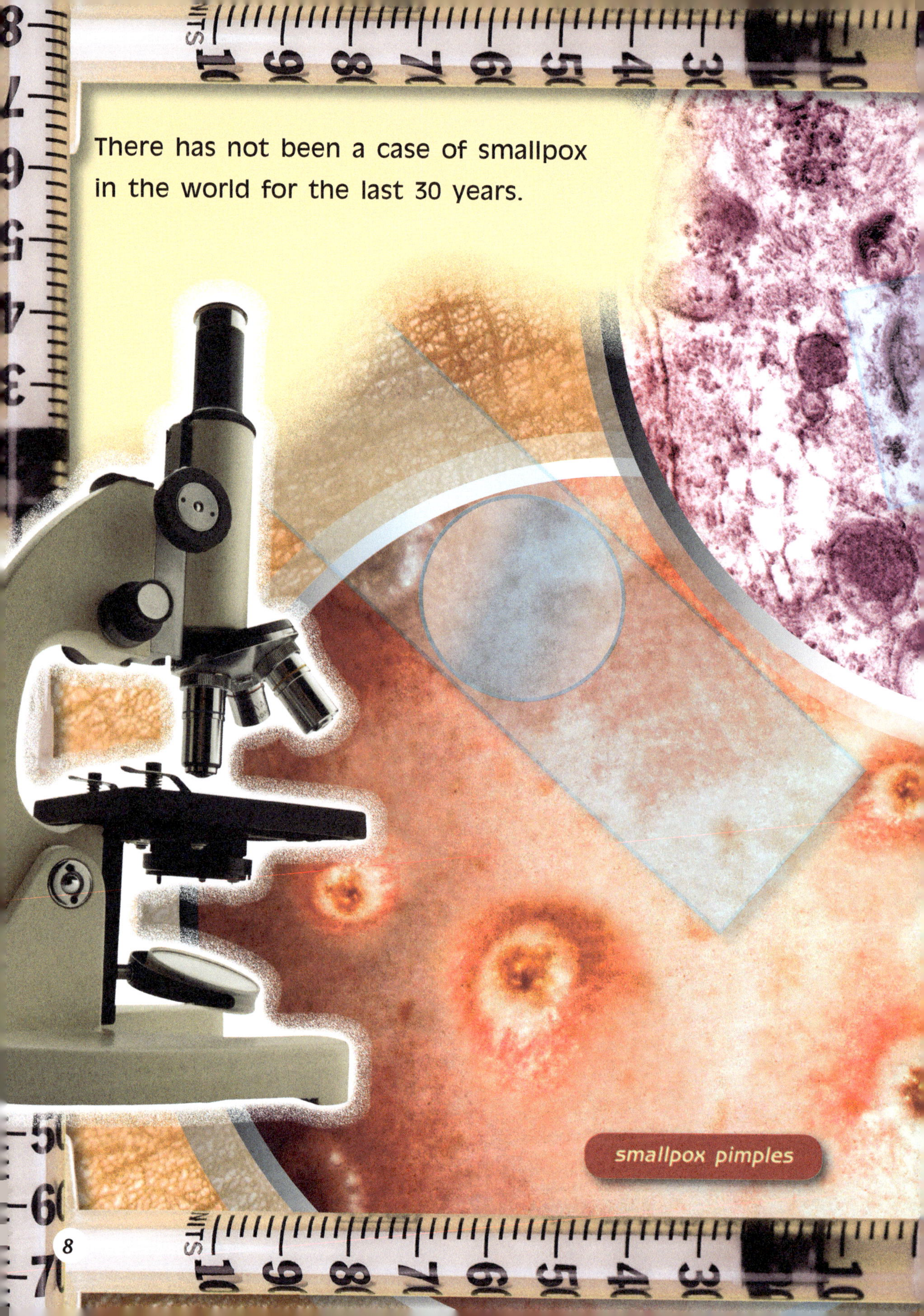

smallpox pimples

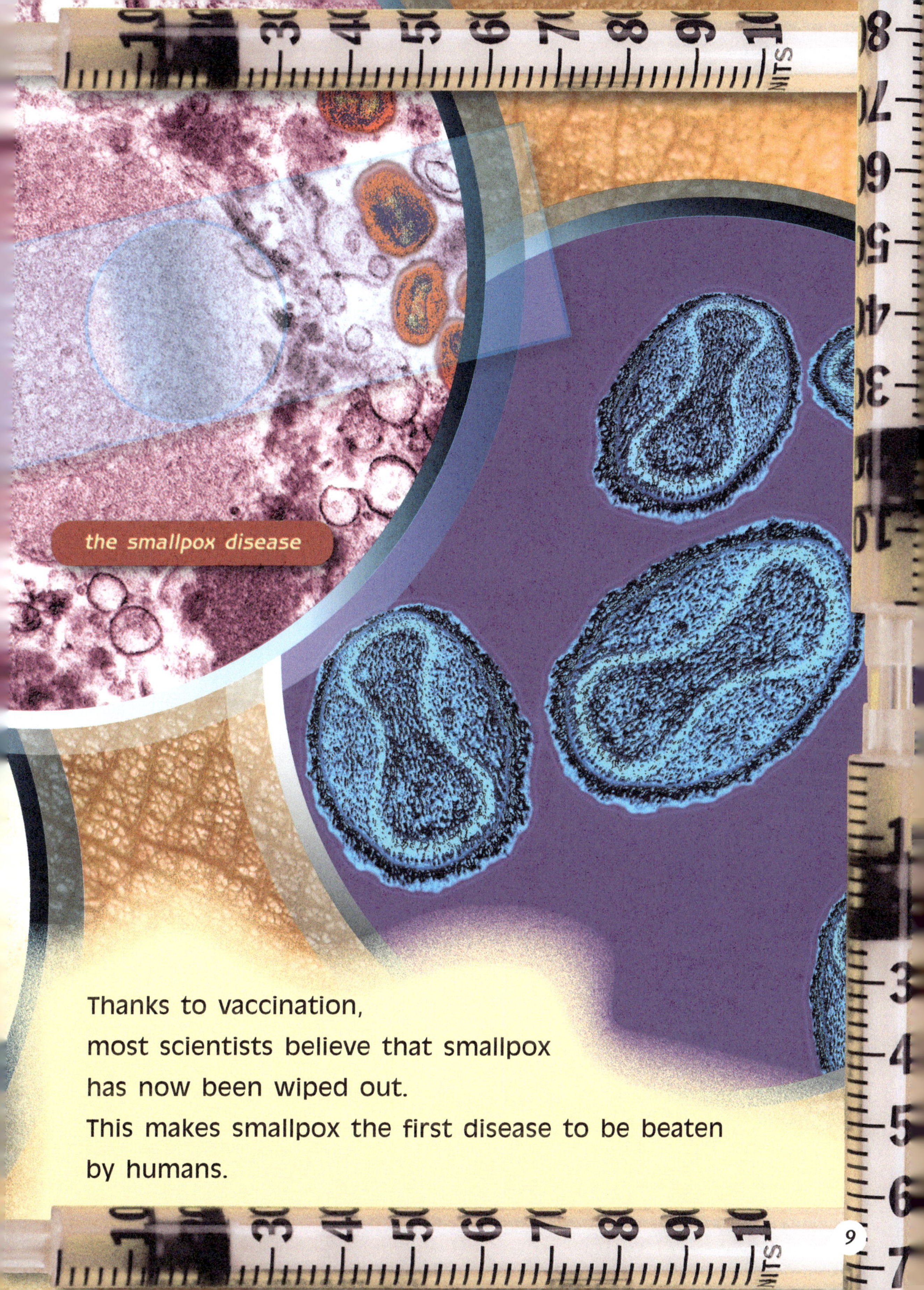

Thanks to vaccination,
most scientists believe that smallpox
has now been wiped out.
This makes smallpox the first disease to be beaten
by humans.

IMMUNITY

In the early 1700s,
an English woman, Mary Montagu,
was living in Turkey.
Smallpox was everywhere,
and many people died from it.

Mary Montagu

Running Words 156

Lady Montagu saw that many Turkish people seemed to be **immune** from smallpox. When she looked into this, she found that Turkish people had found a way to protect themselves against the disease.

Turkish people knew that people only got smallpox once.
So, they used a simple kind of vaccination.
They took some of the material from smallpox pimples and injected it into people who didn't have the disease.

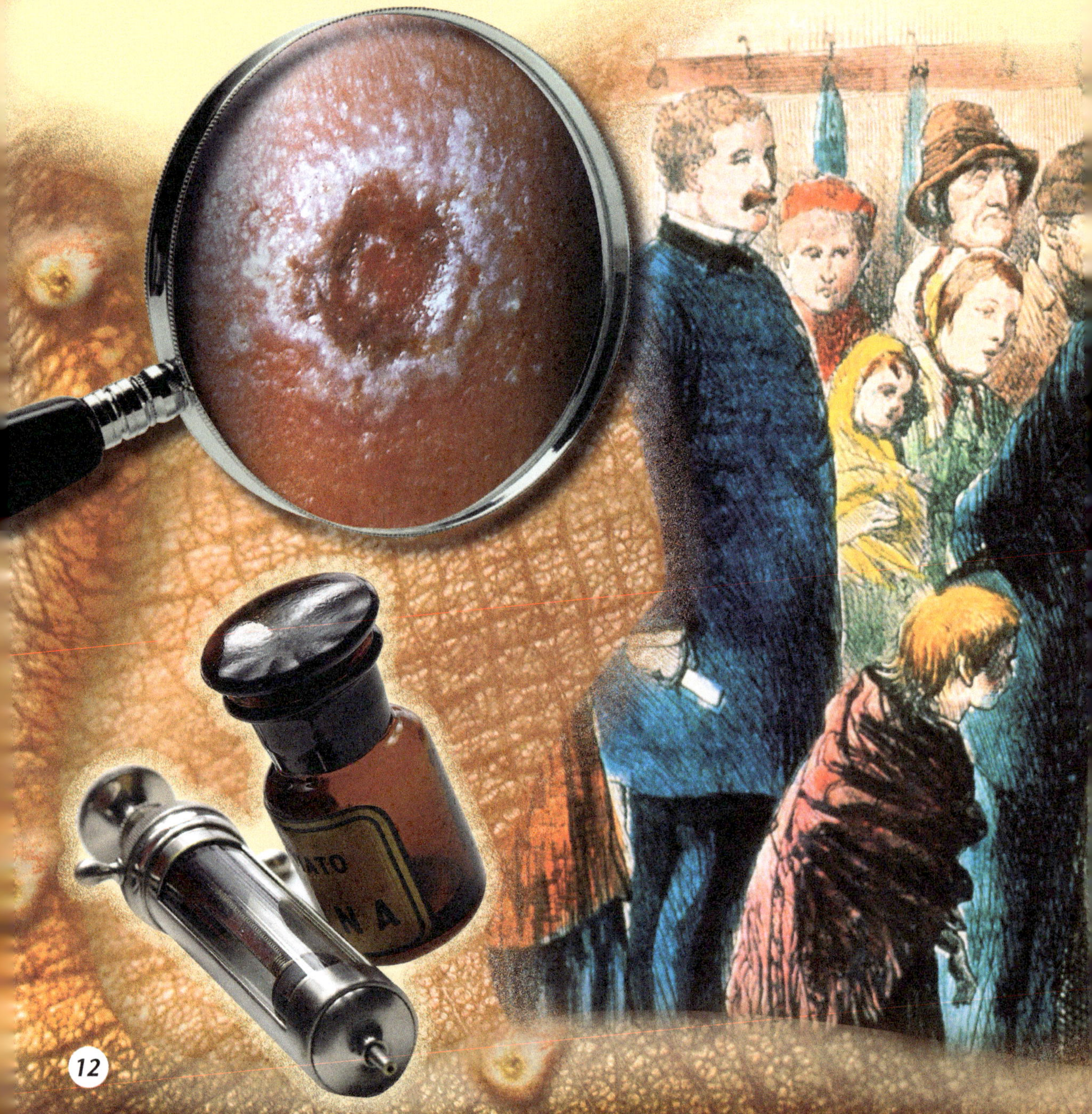

Although this material made the well people sick,
they usually got better quickly,
and they never got smallpox again.

Mary Montagu used this kind of immunisation on her own children.
She told many of her friends in England about it.
Many people in Europe also began to use this kind of immunisation during the 1700s.

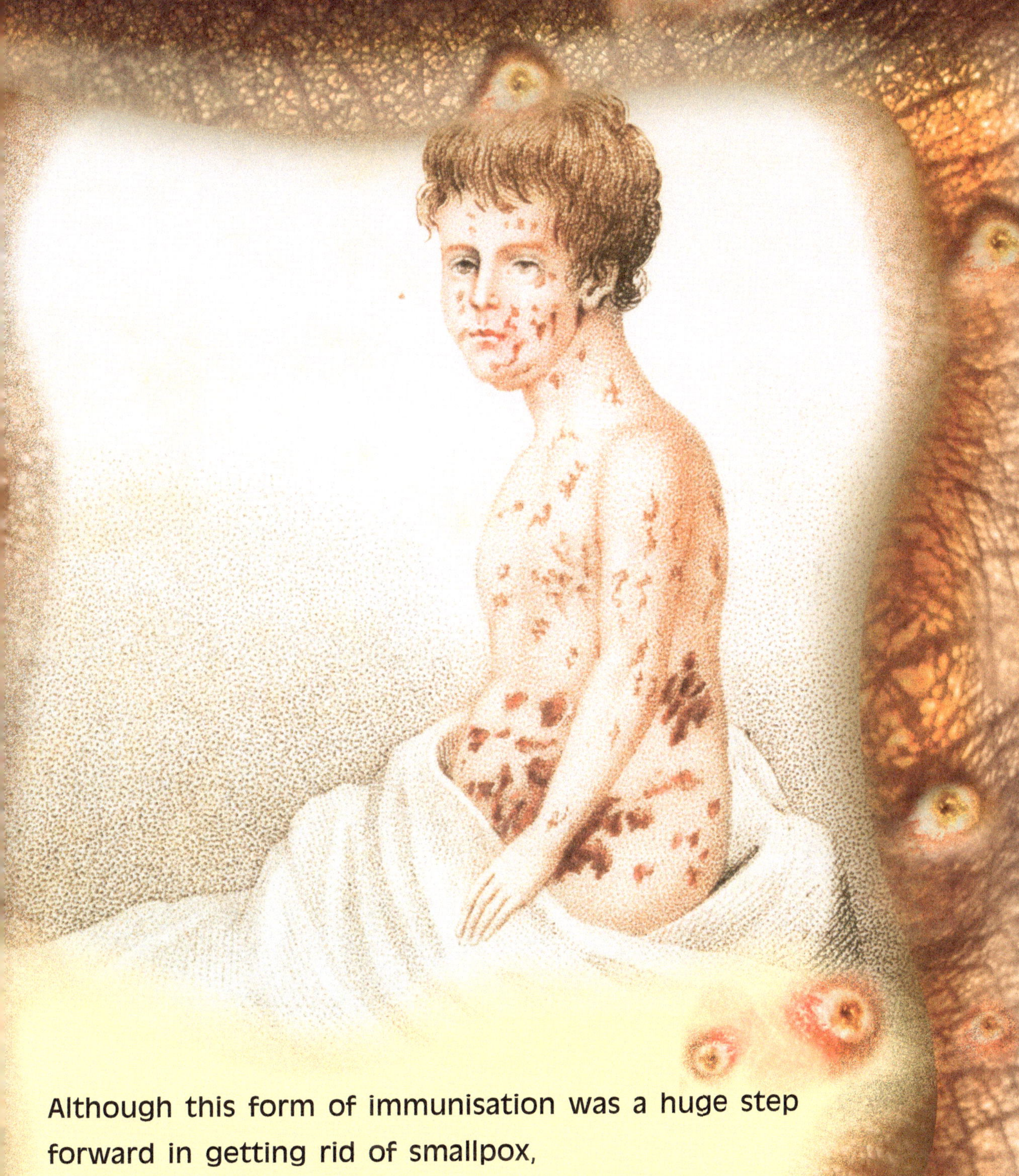

Although this form of immunisation was a huge step forward in getting rid of smallpox, it was not always safe. There was a chance that people would die when the smallpox material was injected into them.

Chapter 4

A BETTER WAY

In the 1790s, Edward Jenner, a doctor in England, saw a lot of people with smallpox.
He also saw a lot of people with a disease called **cowpox**, which was like a mild kind of smallpox.

Dr Edward Jenner

Jenner saw that the people who got cowpox didn't get smallpox.

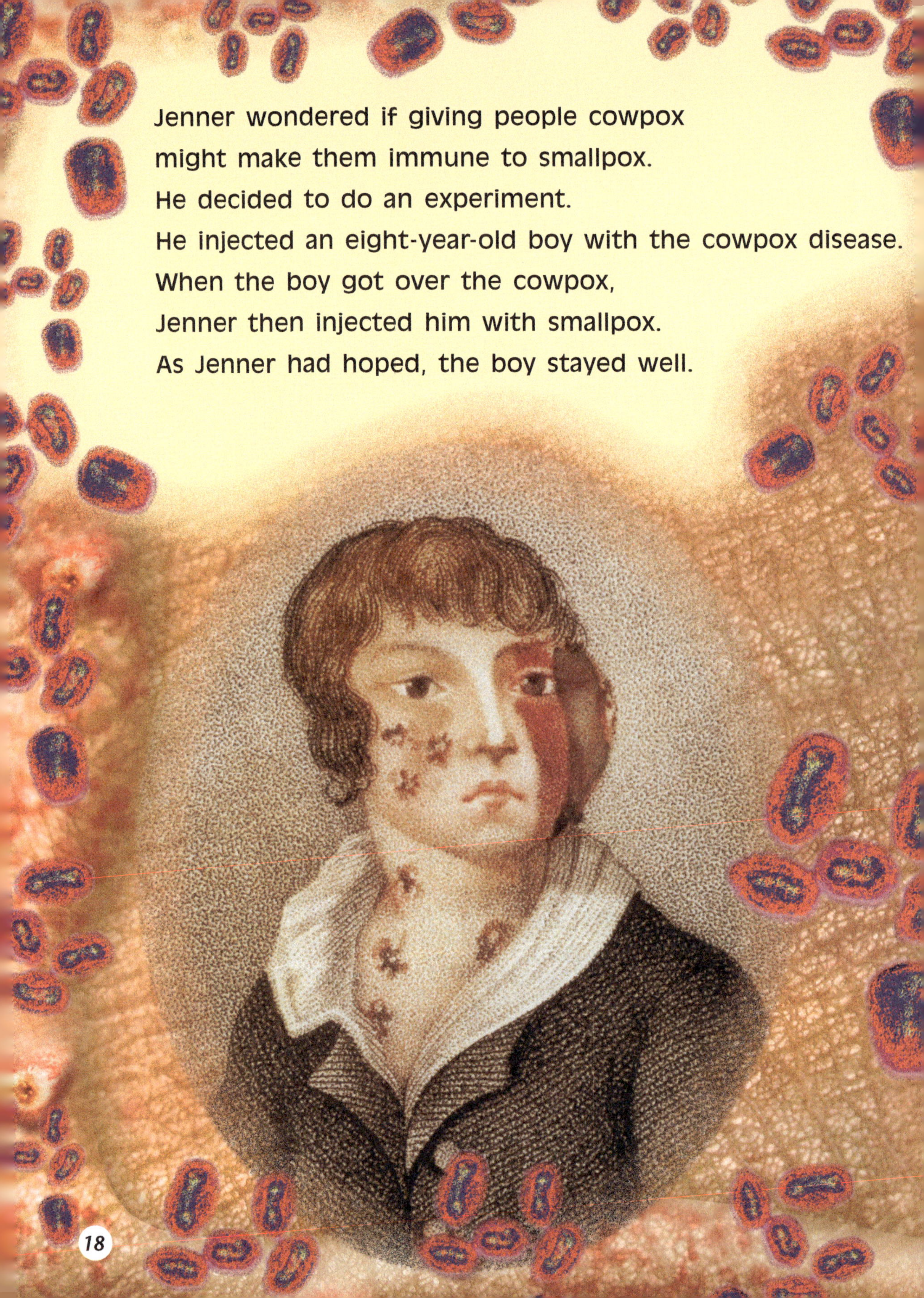

Jenner wondered if giving people cowpox
might make them immune to smallpox.
He decided to do an experiment.
He injected an eight-year-old boy with the cowpox disease.
When the boy got over the cowpox,
Jenner then injected him with smallpox.
As Jenner had hoped, the boy stayed well.

The word vaccine comes from the Latin word *vacca*, which means cow.

Chapter 5

SMALLPOX DISAPPEARS

Jenner had found a safe way to immunise against smallpox. Over the next hundred years, this kind of immunisation began to be used around the world.

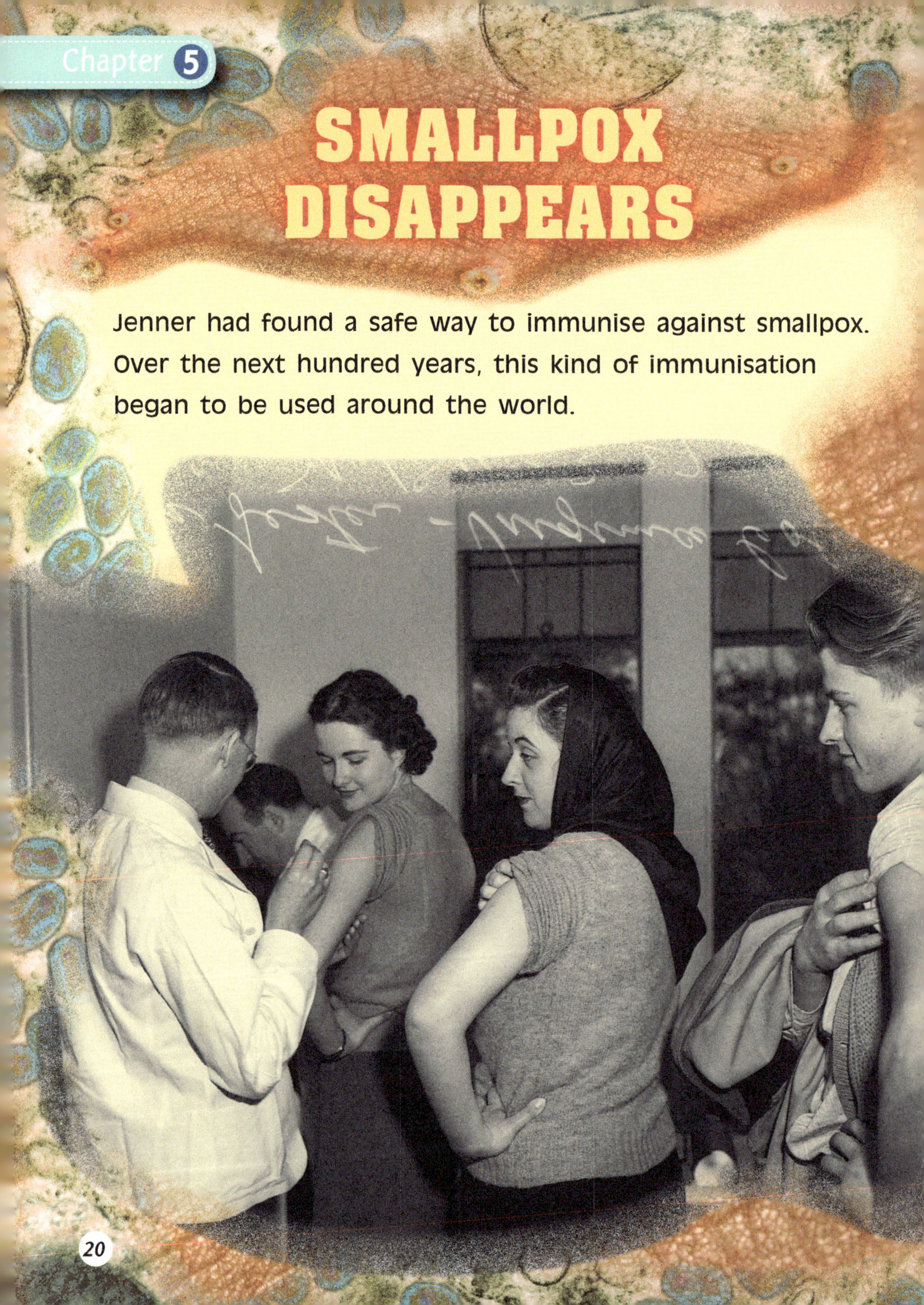

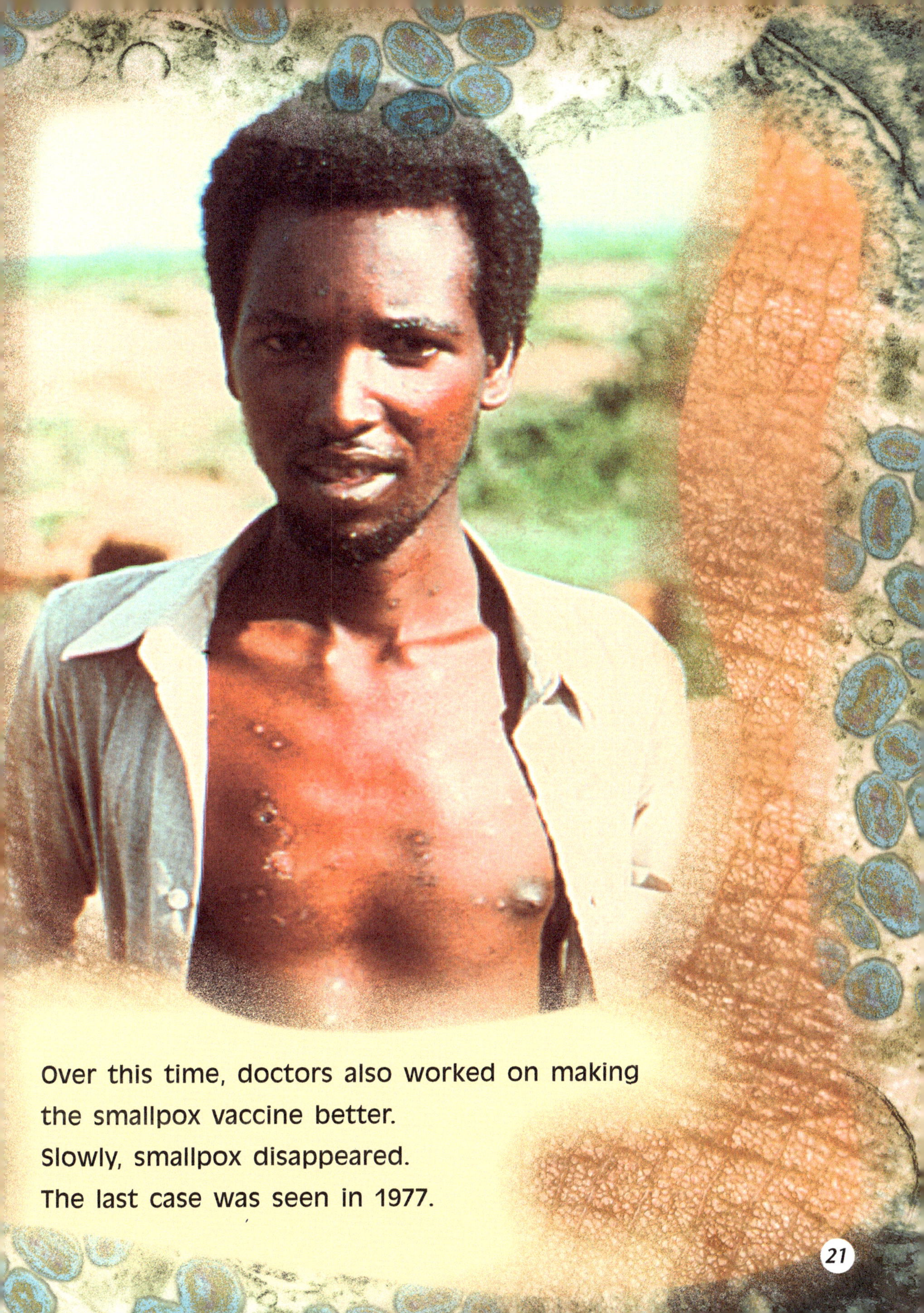

Over this time, doctors also worked on making the smallpox vaccine better.

Slowly, smallpox disappeared.

The last case was seen in 1977.

Many other vaccines were made for other diseases, following on from Jenner's work.
Now, people are protected from many diseases that they would once have died from.
Along with keeping clean and the use of antibiotics, vaccination has made life much better and longer for many people around the world today.

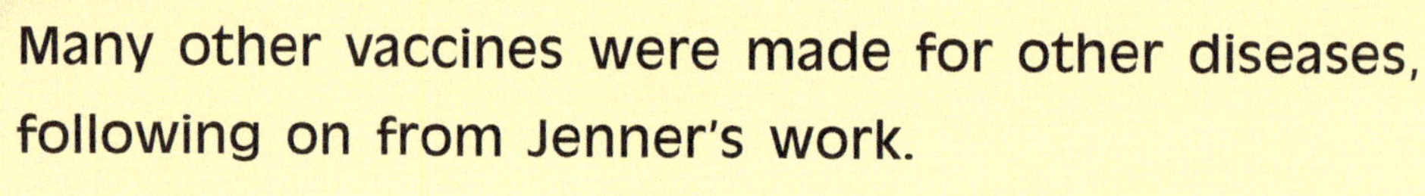

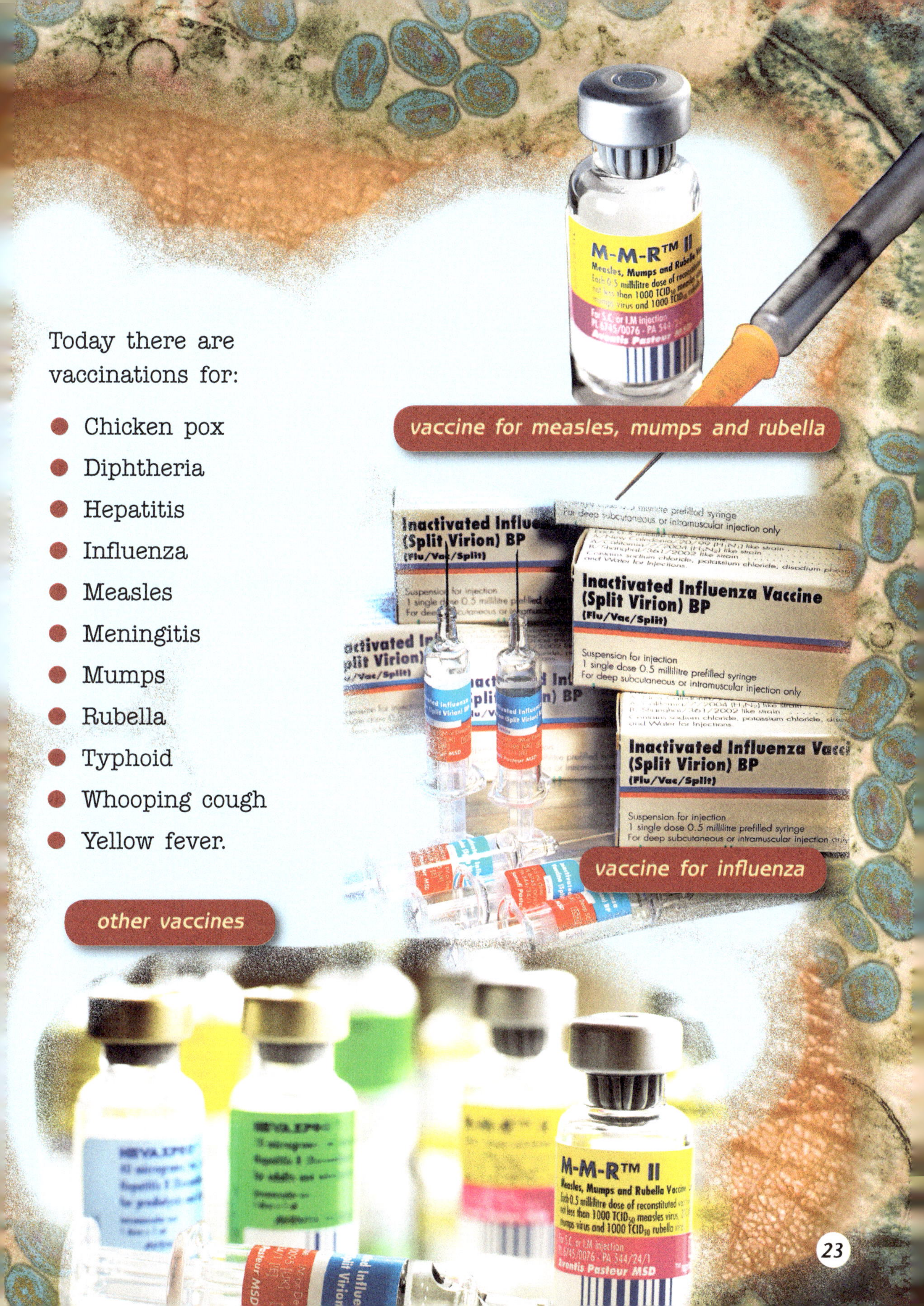

Today there are vaccinations for:

- Chicken pox
- Diphtheria
- Hepatitis
- Influenza
- Measles
- Meningitis
- Mumps
- Rubella
- Typhoid
- Whooping cough
- Yellow fever.

vaccine for measles, mumps and rubella

vaccine for influenza

other vaccines

Glossary

antibiotics medicine that kills or slows the growth of bacteria

cowpox a disease of the skin caused by a virus

disease an abnormal condition of the body or mind that causes discomfort, dysfunction or distress

immune resistant to disease

immunity protection

vaccination a treatment to provide protection from a disease

vaccines medicines used to provide protection from disease

Index